SHERLOCK

The Sign of Three

by ... Sign of Three'
... Steve Thompson

Based on the story 'The Sign of the Four'
by Sir Arthur Conan Doyle

LEVEL 2

■SCHOLASTIC

Adapted by: Fiona Beddall

Publisher: Jacquie Bloese

Editor: Fiona Davis

Designer: Dawn Wilson

Picture research: Pupak Navabpour

Photo credits:
Page 5: D. Dennison/Getty Images.
Page 48: Dark Side/SXC.hu.
Pages 50 & 51: Imagno, Archive Photos/Getty Images;
Warner Brothers/Allstar.

Published by Scholastic Ltd. 2015

Mary Glasgow Magazines (Scholastic Ltd.)
Euston House
24 Eversholt Street
London NW1 IDB

Printed in Malaysia

Reprinted in 2017

CONTENTS	PAGE

THE SIGN OF THREE

SHERLOCK HOLMES solves crimes. He has a very clever, logical mind, but he doesn't always understand people's emotions.

JOHN WATSON was an army doctor in Afghanistan. When he came back to England, he started working with Sherlock. They became very good friends.

MARY MORSTAN

is John's girlfriend and is soon going to be his wife. All their friends have invitations to the wedding.

DETECTIVE INSPECTOR LESTRADE is

in the London police. Sherlock often helps him with his cases.

MAJOR JAMES SHOLTO was in

the army with John. The Major left the army a few years ago.

MRS HUDSON

owns Sherlock's flat. She lives downstairs from him.

PLACES

221B Baker Street **This is** Sherlock's address in London.

The Queen lives in Buckingham Palace when she is in London.

JANINE HAWKINS is

Mary's best friend. She would like to be married, but she doesn't have a boyfriend.

STEPHEN BAINBRIDGE is a

young man in the army. He is a guard at Buckingham Palace.

CHAPTER 1
'Help me'

'Today is a good day,' said Detective Inspector Lestrade.

'Not for the Waters family,' smiled the policewoman next to him.

The Waters family were famous for their crimes in London. They took thousands of pounds from banks and the police could never stop them. They always left before the police arrived.

But today was different. After months of planning, Lestrade was ready for them. The Waters family were inside a bank, and there were police all around it.

'Nothing can go wrong this time,' said the policewoman. 'We've put ten men on top of the building, and another two on Mafeking Road. There are …'

'Sorry,' said Lestrade. He had a new text message. 'Let me just read this.'

HELP.
BAKER ST.
NOW.

The message said: *HELP. BAKER STREET. NOW.*

Lestrade only knew one person in Baker Street: Sherlock Holmes. Sherlock wasn't a policeman, but he solved a lot of difficult cases for the police.

There was another text message: *HELP ME. PLEASE.*

This was important. Sherlock was in trouble. 'I'm sorry,' Lestrade said to the policewoman. 'I have to go. You can take the Waters family to the police station for me.'

'But if you go now, no one is going to know about your hard work. This is *your* case, Detective Inspector. You can't just leave.'

But Lestrade wasn't there. He was already on his way to Sherlock. 'I need men, lots of men, at Baker Street!' he shouted into his mobile.

A few minutes later, Lestrade ran into Sherlock's flat.

'Sherlock! What's wrong?'

Sherlock was in front of his computer.

'This is difficult,' he said slowly. 'It's the most difficult thing that I've ever done.'

'What is?' asked Lestrade as ten police cars arrived in the street.

'I'm the best man* at John's wedding tomorrow, and I have to make a speech. Do you know any funny stories about him?'

---

* At a man's wedding, his best friend is his best man. The best man's speech is an important part of a wedding day.

CHAPTER 2
The big day

'So, today's the big day!' said Mrs Hudson happily as she gave Sherlock his morning cup of tea. She owned his flat and often cooked and cleaned for him.

'What big day?' asked Sherlock. 'John and Mary already live together. Today they're going to say some words in church, have a party, and leave on a short holiday. After that they're going to live together again. What's big about that?'

'When you're married, things change,' said Mrs Hudson. 'You don't understand, Sherlock, because you live alone. My best friend, Margaret, and I were always very close. We planned to be friends all our lives. But after my wedding, I only saw her a few times. It was sad, but …'

'Biscuits, Mrs Hudson!' said Sherlock. 'You always bring me biscuits in the morning.'

'Well, I haven't got any, so …'

'Don't they have any at the shops, Mrs Hudson? Biscuits! Now!'

'Oh, Sherlock! I'm going to talk to your mother about you,' Mrs Hudson said sadly as she walked out of the door.

Sherlock looked at her empty chair. John always sat in that chair when he was in the flat. John … Sherlock's only friend. Was Mrs Hudson right? Was this wedding the end of his time with John?

* * *

John and Mary walked happily out of the church with Sherlock next to them. They were married!

'Can I have a photo of just the two of you?' asked the photographer.

Sherlock smiled for the camera.

'Just John and Mary?' said the photographer.

Sherlock didn't move.

'Sherlock, can you stand over there?' said John quietly.

'Oh, sorry!' said Sherlock as he moved away.

He wasn't alone for long.

'The famous Mr Holmes! It's nice to meet you,' said a young woman with long dark hair. It was Mary's friend, Janine. 'I've heard that women often meet their future husband at a wedding. Do you think it's true?'

'I'm sorry?' said Sherlock. What was she talking about?

'I was saying, do you think people fall in love at weddings?'

Sherlock never had girlfriends. Crimes were more interesting than women.

'If you're looking for love, talk to the man in the blue jacket. He's a doctor and his wife left him a few months ago.'

Sherlock didn't know the man, but little things told him a lot. He looked at the man's shoes. 'He lives in a nice old house in the country, but …'

'What?' asked Janine.

'His wife left him because he had lots of girlfriends. He's not the right man for you.'

Janine moved closer to Sherlock. 'Mr Holmes,' she said, 'you're going to be very useful.'

* * *

The guests arrived at the hotel for the wedding lunch. John, Mary and their best man, Sherlock, were at the door of the dining room as people went in.

An eight-year-old boy threw his arms around Sherlock.

'Hello, Archie,' said Sherlock. 'You were very quiet in the church. Good boy!'

'Thank you for talking to him before everything started,' said Archie's mother. 'It was a big help.'

Archie smiled as he remembered their talk before the wedding – about solving crimes.

'And you have some photos for him, I think?' continued his mother.

'Yes, if he's good during the speeches.'

'Photos of bodies with no heads!' said Archie happily.

Sherlock looked quickly at Archie's mother. 'It's a lovely hotel, isn't it?' he said loudly.

Archie went into the dining room with his mother.

'What did you just say?' she asked Archie.

John gave Sherlock a funny look as he and Mary followed Sherlock into the dining room. They each took a drink, and Mary also took some food.

'I'm so hungry!' she said. 'But it's a bad idea. I'm already too fat for this dress!'

Janine came to talk to Sherlock again.

'He's nice!' Janine said as a man walked past them. 'What do you think?'

'Yes, but he's changed his shirt from the one that he was wearing in church,' said Sherlock. 'The clean shirt is already wet under the arms. I think he has a problem …'

'OK, thanks for telling me!' said Janine. 'What about his friend?'

'He's married, but he often meets other women.'

'How do you know that?'

'Look carefully at his mobile. He uses that phone in the shower. He talks to his girlfriends there.'

'You're clever!' said Janine. 'Can I keep you?'

'Do you enjoy solving crimes?' asked Sherlock.

'Why? Are you looking for someone to work with you?' asked Janine.

Sherlock looked at John. He didn't need anyone while his friend worked with him. But for how much longer did he have John?

In another part of the room, Mary talked to John about his friend, Major James Sholto.

'Is he here?' she asked.

'No,' said John sadly, 'but I'm not surprised. He doesn't often go out these days.'

A minute later, a tall man in army uniform walked into the room. He was older than John and had a bad left arm.

'It's Major Sholto!' said John happily. 'He came!'

'It's good to see you, John,' said Sholto. 'Is life outside the army going well?'

'Yes, thanks, as you can see! And what about you? Where are you living these days?'

'Oh, out in the country. It's a small place – no one's ever heard of it.'

Sherlock watched them. 'If John and Major Sholto are close friends,' he asked Mary, 'why does John never talk about him?'

'He talks to me about him all the time. But it's a surprise to see him here. He almost never leaves his house.'

'Really? Why's that?'

'He had a terrible time in the army, poor man. The last time he was in Afghanistan, he had lots of brave young men with him, but they all died out there. Only Sholto came home. The dead men's families were very angry with him. Some people wanted *him* dead too.'

Mary had some of her drink.

'Yeuch! This drink is terrible! It wasn't like this when I tried it in the shop!'

CHAPTER 3
The Guard in the Shower

'I'm going to start with some emails,' said Sherlock loudly to everyone at the wedding. It was the end of dinner and time for the best man's speech.

'Dear Mr and Mrs Watson,' read Sherlock. 'I'm so sorry I can't be with you on your special day. Good luck, from Mike.'

There was a smile from the people in the room who knew Mike.

'To John and Mary. We're so happy for you! Have a great day. With love and ...' Sherlock made a strange face. '... lots of big hugs from Stella and Ted.' Why were people so emotional about weddings?

Some of the guests, including Mrs Hudson, laughed at Sherlock's face, but he tried to continue.

'Good luck, my ...' Sherlock stopped again. Did he really have to say this? '... my sweet, lovely girl.' More people were laughing now. 'Lots of love from Cam.'

Sherlock wanted to finish this part of his speech
as quickly as possible. He was sure that no one was
interested in these stupid emails!

'Special day …' he said for the next message, and
hurried to another. 'Very special day …' And the next
three. 'Love … Lots of love … Love.' He quickly finished
all the messages. 'They're all the same. People love John
and Mary. Not very interesting!'

No one spoke for a moment. This wasn't like other
wedding speeches!

'John,' continued Sherlock in a different voice. 'John
Watson. My friend.' He looked at John and John smiled
back. 'I'm sorry. I can't say that this wedding is a good
idea. I believe in logic, not emotion, and … well, weddings
are all about love. Too much emotion and no logic at all.
Only stupid people enjoy weddings.'

John and Mary didn't look happy. There were a lot of angry faces in the room now.

'When John asked me to be his best man, I was very surprised,' said Sherlock. 'As you can see, I'm a terrible man. I always say the wrong thing and upset people. So I never thought that I could be anyone's best friend – and certainly not the best friend of the kindest and bravest person that I have ever known.

'John, you say that I'm your best friend. Well, I can't tell you that you've made a good choice. But today you've made another choice, and this time it's a brilliant one. Mary, you and John are going to be fantastic together.'

Now a few people in the room were crying. Mrs Hudson was the loudest.

'What's happened, John?' Sherlock asked quietly. 'Why are they doing that? Have I said something wrong?'

'No, you haven't,' said John. He knew that Sherlock didn't like showing emotion, but John stood up and gave Sherlock a hug. Everyone smiled.

Sherlock continued with his speech.

'Now it's time for some stories about John. For those, we don't have to look very far. He writes them himself! He has written a blog about lots of our cases, and we've certainly had some strange ones. Today I'm going to talk about one of the most interesting: the Guard in the Shower.

'It all started with a letter. *Dear Mr Holmes,* the letter said, *My name's Bainbridge and I'm in the army. I'm one of the Queen's Guard. I'm writing to you because someone keeps following me. I'm really worried about it. I stand outside Buckingham Palace and there are always lots of people there. They're from all over the world. They come up to me and take photos. That's fine – it's just part of the job. But this is different. Someone is following me all the time. He's watching every move that I make. He takes photos of me when I'm working. He even takes photos through the window when I'm in my bedroom.*

'I was interested in Bainbridge's letter from the start. Lots of people like taking photos of the guards outside Buckingham Palace. But there are forty men in the Queen's Guard. Why was the man taking photos of Bainbridge but not of the other guards?

'John and I went to the home of the Queen's Guard near Buckingham Palace to find out more. Bainbridge had another hour of work before we could talk to him.

'We looked around the outside of the building for a bit, but then we met Bainbridge's boss, Major Reed. He wasn't a very helpful man.

"Why does Bainbridge need a detective?" he asked when he found out my job. "If there's a problem, he must talk to me. We don't have secrets in the Queen's Guard."

'Suddenly, a guard ran towards us. "It's Bainbridge, Major! He's dead!"

'We all ran after the guard to the shower room and saw Bainbridge on the floor. There was blood and glass everywhere.

"I had to break the shower door," said the guard to explain the glass. "But I couldn't do anything to help him."

'John wanted to look at the body, but the Major had other ideas. He pointed at me and John and shouted, "Take those men to the police! They murdered Bainbridge!"

'He wasn't very clever, this Major. "What weapon did we use to murder him?" I asked. "Have we got a weapon?"

"Bainbridge was outside Buckingham Palace five minutes ago," said John. "We didn't have time to kill him. We were with you."

'But the Major wasn't listening. "You clearly killed him before he went into the shower."

"No, that's impossible," I explained. "Look at his hair. He was washing it when he died. He started his shower, and *then* someone killed him."

"Bainbridge – or *someone* anyway – locked the shower from the inside," said the guard who found the body. "I had to break it to open it."

"You climbed over the shower door!" the Major said to me.

"Really?" I asked. "How could I do that and stay dry? You can see that I'm not wet."

"Major, please!" shouted John. "I'm a doctor. I worked for three years with the army in Afghanistan. Please let me look at this body."

'The Major was quiet for a few moments. Finally, he moved back so John could look at Bainbridge.

'I started thinking hard. Bainbridge didn't kill himself. He had no weapon. So how did it happen? I was excited. I love solving this kind of crime. It's good exercise for the mind.

'While I was thinking about the crime, John found a wound in Bainbridge's back.

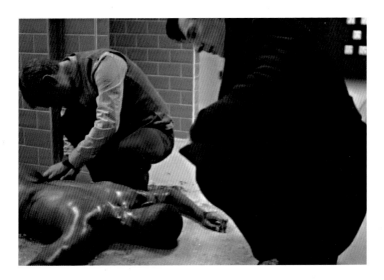

"It's really small," he said. Then he stopped. "Sherlock!" he said. "He isn't dead!"

'Of course, after that there were lots of phone calls, nurses, hospitals … . But in those first important moments, John was brilliant. He stopped the blood, and because of him, Bainbridge didn't die. He's going to be working back at Buckingham Palace again soon.

'Bainbridge didn't die, but that doesn't change the facts of the case. This guard stood outside Buckingham Palace for hours. Lots of people were there, and there was nothing wrong with him. But five minutes later, he was almost dead in a shower. A shower with a door that someone locked from the inside. And no weapon. What kind of weapon can just disappear? And what kind of killer can walk through walls? It was a clever crime … very clever. But in all of this, there was only one thing that was really brilliant. And what was that? John Watson. While I was trying to solve a crime, John saved a life. He's not only brave and kind. He can also do stuff.'

Everyone in the room laughed. John tried hard not to cry.

'But I'm not here today just to say nice things about John,' continued Sherlock. 'I'm also going to tell you some of his secrets.'

'But wait a minute!' shouted Detective Inspector Lestrade. 'What happened to Bainbridge?'

'Well …' said Sherlock. 'I'm sorry, but I don't know.' His face went a bit red. 'I didn't solve that case. It happens sometimes.'

CHAPTER 4
The Man for One Day

'This next story shows a different side to Mary's new husband,' continued Sherlock. 'A woman, Tessa, visited us one evening to tell us about her love life. It was very boring. John and I both fell asleep. Tessa's story started when she met a man, Tim. They had a meal together in his flat. They talked. They laughed. Then she never heard from him again – the usual thing.

'But Tessa was surprised, and she went back to his flat a few days later. There was no sign of him there. She spoke to the woman in the flat next to his and found out something strange.

"Tim died two weeks ago," the woman said.

'Tessa started to believe that the man was a ghost. On the Internet, she found a website for people who told the same kind of story.

'Now the case was starting to sound interesting. John and I agreed to go with Tessa to Tim's flat. But the new owner wasn't happy.

"I'm calling the police!" he said angrily.

"No, no, don't do that!" said Tessa. "This is the famous detective, Sherlock Holmes, and his partner, John Hamish Watson. They're here to solve a crime for me."

'Tessa kept talking, but the man didn't want to listen. In the end, he pushed us out. But I can work quickly. By then, I already knew that there was nothing important in the flat.

'The next job was to look at the website. I read hundreds of "ghost date" stories. Most of them were very boring. But I found four that I was interested in.

'There were differences between the four stories. Gail met a blond man, Oscar, in a pub. Charlotte met a man with long dark hair, Mike, in a sports centre. Robyn met Terry (red hair – she loves red hair) on the bus. Vicky met her man on the Internet, and his name was "Love Monkey". They all had a date at their new boyfriend's flat – a different address in each case. Each woman had a lovely evening, and then never saw the man again. The most interesting thing was this: the dates were on the Monday, Tuesday, Wednesday and Thursday of the same week. Tessa had her date on the Friday.

'This couldn't just be luck. I felt sure that the five women were talking about the same man. I called him the Man for One Day. I looked at the obituaries in that week's newspaper, and I was right! All the men's names and addresses were in the obituaries! A man borrowed a dead, unmarried man's name and flat for one evening only and had a date there. The next evening, he had a new name, different hair, a new flat and a different woman. But why? Why does anyone go to all that trouble? What was he looking for?

'I asked Tessa and the other women about their jobs – a nurse, a gardener, a cook, a cleaner, a guard. At first I thought that they worked for the same person. But no, they all had jobs with different businesses. They didn't have the same hobbies. They didn't like the same kinds of men. For a long time I couldn't understand it.

'But there was one interesting thing about these women. I asked them, "Do you have a secret that you've never told anyone?"

'Very quickly, all five women answered, "No!"

'Strange. You see, everyone has secrets. Everyone. Then none of them answered my messages again. Even Tessa, the woman who never stopped talking, suddenly had to go. "Goodbye," she said. "Enjoy the wedding!"

'Was there something about their secrets that joined the women in some way? But what? And why did the man never see them again?

'John thought the answer was clear. "He's probably married," he said.

'And, you know, John was probably right. This man was trying to escape his boring life with his wife – having boring conversations about her boring job, watching boring shows on TV. He was …'

Suddenly Sherlock saw that no one in the room was smiling. What was wrong now? Oh! he thought. This was not a good way to talk about married men at a wedding.

'Maybe I haven't chosen the right case to talk about,' said Sherlock. 'I'll stop now.'

'Yes, please stop!' said John.

'You see …' continued Sherlock. 'I can understand all

the signs that people leave after a crime. But only John can understand people. I can solve your crime. But you'll need John to save your life. I know that, because he's saved my life many times, in many different ways.'

Sherlock thought about some of those times now. In crime work, you were never far from a gun, a knife, a dangerous killer. And in quiet weeks, there was the danger of being bored. For Sherlock, that was worse than any dangers in the outside world. Having John at his side made a big difference.

Sherlock looked again at the people in the room. They were waiting for him to finish his speech.

'John's blog is the story of two men and their adventures,' he continued. 'But from today there's a new story, a bigger adventure.' He looked at John and Mary. 'Everyone, please take your glasses and drink to the adventure of married life. Mary Elizabeth Watson and John Hamish Watson, we ...'

Sherlock stopped suddenly. The photographer took photos of him as he stood there. Everyone waited. Sherlock's glass fell from his hand and hit the floor with a crash.

CHAPTER 5
'It's you!'

Sherlock was thinking fast. He was remembering Tessa's words in Tim's flat: 'Sherlock Holmes and John *Hamish* Watson'. But no one knew John's middle name! He never told it to anyone because he hated it so much. Even Sherlock, his best friend, didn't know it for years. Sherlock only found out when Mary wanted to include 'Hamish' on the wedding invitation. John hated that idea, but in the end, he agreed.

And Sherlock remembered another strange thing. When he last talked to Tessa, she said, 'Enjoy the wedding!' But he and John didn't tell her about the wedding. That meant that she knew from someone else – someone who had a wedding invitation!

John and Mary only sent invitations to about a hundred people. So it couldn't just be luck. The Man for One Day wanted to meet Tessa because she knew about the wedding. And that could only mean that he wanted to be at the wedding too.

It was all clear to Sherlock now. The Man for One Day was in the room at that moment, and he was planning something bad. Sherlock had to stop him. He had to find the man.

Everyone was still looking at Sherlock. They were waiting for the end of his speech. But he couldn't finish it yet. He had to find the Man for One Day while everyone was in the room.

Sherlock started walking around as he tried to continue the speech.

'Who wants to go to a wedding? Who wants to go even when it's a lot of trouble?'

He was speaking fast, and everyone could hear the worry in his voice. But then he remembered the guests and changed his voice to a happy one.

'Who wants to go to a wedding? All of us, of course!' he said with an empty smile. 'Weddings are great!'

'Something's wrong,' John said quietly to Mary.

'I could talk to you all night about John,' continued Sherlock. 'He always wears … er … interesting clothes.'

The people at the tables were starting to look uncomfortable. This was a strange wedding speech.

'And he can cook. Did you know that?' said Sherlock.

Who was the Man for One Day? Sherlock couldn't think. There were too many people at the wedding. How could Sherlock find the man in this big group?

'Too many, too many, too many!' Sherlock shouted angrily.

The wedding guests were looking frightened now.

'Sorry!' said Sherlock. 'Too many good things about John! I can't tell you about all of them. Right, what was I saying? I wanted to talk about …'

The Man for One Day worked so hard to be here. He lied. He changed the colour of his hair. He borrowed the flats of dead men. Why? Why was this wedding so important to him? Suddenly, Sherlock knew. He was certain.

'… murder!' he shouted.

Sherlock saw the guests' frightened faces.

'Sorry, no, not murder! I wanted to talk about married life, not murder. They're almost the same, really. They both end when someone is dead. But murder's quicker.'

This wasn't the right thing to say at a wedding, of course. But he needed more time. And what else could he talk about?

'John can sing really well too … or quite well,' said Sherlock.

Sherlock was holding his mobile behind his back. He sent a text message to Lestrade. He also said quietly in Lestrade's ear, 'Greg, go to the toilets now, please.'

'Why do I have to do that?' asked the police detective angrily.

Lestrade looked at the new message from Sherlock on his mobile: *Don't let anyone out of this building*.

'OK ... in fact I will go to the toilets,' Lestrade said, and walked quickly out of the room.

Who was the Man for One Day? Sherlock still couldn't answer that. Not you, and not you, he thought as he looked around the room.

'Not you! Not you!' He was shouting again. Finally he pointed to John. 'It's you!'

'What do you mean? What's me?'

'You've given me the answer, John. Again. Don't solve the crime. Save the life.'

Sherlock couldn't find the Man for One Day. But maybe he could find the person that the Man for One Day wanted to kill.

'Let's play a game of murder,' Sherlock said to all the guests.

'Oh, Sherlock!' said Mrs Hudson. 'Why can't you just finish your speech and then everyone can enjoy themselves?'

'Who do you murder at a wedding?' continued Sherlock.

'A lot of people would like to murder you at the moment,' Mrs Hudson answered.

But Sherlock didn't listen. 'More importantly, who can you only kill at a wedding? It's easy to kill people, really. I often plan my friends' murders in my mind, just for fun. But murder is easier somewhere with few people. A wedding is a difficult place to kill someone. So why choose a wedding? It's stupid … or it's your only choice. Maybe you're trying to kill someone that you can't reach in another way. You can't find out the person's address … Or the person has guards at his home and never goes out … Maybe the person knows that he's in danger.'

As Sherlock looked around the room, his eyes rested on the face of Major Sholto. He remembered something from earlier that day. When John asked Sholto about his home, the Major didn't say the name of the place. He almost never left his home. And the families of some of his men wanted him dead. Why didn't Sherlock think of Sholto sooner? It was clear to him now. This was the person that the Man for One Day wanted to kill.

The Man for One Day had dates with all those women: a nurse, a gardener, a cook, a guard, a cleaner. They worked for different businesses, but at some time they all worked in Sholto's house in the country. And they all agreed not to give anyone information about their work there. That was why they said no so quickly to Sherlock's question about a secret.

Sherlock quickly wrote 'It's you!' on a piece of paper and put it in front of Sholto.

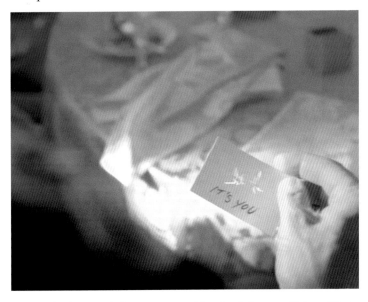

As Sholto read the message, Sherlock kept talking. 'But there's another question, and it's a big one. How do you kill someone at a wedding? There are so many people here. How do you do it and then escape?'

'Mr Holmes! Mr Holmes!' said a little voice.

'Oh, hello!' said Sherlock to the boy. 'Have you got an idea? If you're right, I'll show you some more of those photos.'

'I know someone who could do it!' said Archie. 'The man who can walk through walls. The man who can kill without a weapon.'

Sherlock didn't understand.

'The man who tried to kill the Guard in the Shower!' continued Archie.

Sherlock thought about this idea. Yes! Brilliant! Archie was right! The Man for One Day didn't just plan today's murder. He practised it too. The Guard in the Shower case was a practice for the murder of Major Sholto!

CHAPTER 6
'Solve it, Sherlock!'

Sherlock had to work fast.

'I'm sorry, everyone,' he said loudly. 'We have to stop the wedding speeches for a few minutes. We'll be back soon.'

Then he turned to John and Mary. 'The Man for One Day is going to murder Major Sholto,' he said quietly. 'When and how? I don't know. But it's going to happen.'

'And who's the Man for One Day?' John asked.

'I don't know that either,' replied Sherlock.

He looked for Major Sholto, but the Major wasn't there.

'He just walked out,' said John.

Sherlock ran out of the room.

'Stay here!' John said to Mary.

John ran after Sherlock, but he found him on the stairs.

'Come on! Let's go!' said John. 'Which is Sholto's room?'

'I don't know,' answered Sherlock.

'What do you mean, you don't know? You remember everything!'

But Sherlock really didn't know. They were losing time, and every minute was important.

'Room 207!' shouted Mary as she ran past them. The men followed her up the stairs.

* * *

In his hotel bedroom, Major Sholto used his one good hand to lock the door and open his travel bag. From the bag, he took out a gun. He could hear people outside the door, but they couldn't get in.

'Major Sholto!' shouted Sherlock. He was hitting the door.

'You say that someone is trying to kill me,' said the Major. 'It won't be the first time. I'm ready.'

'Major, please open the door!' said John.

'Break down the door!' said Mary.

'That's not a good idea,' said the Major. 'I have a gun in my hand. I've used it before, and I'll use it again.'

'But you're not safe in there, Major,' said Sherlock. 'A lock didn't stop the killer before. It won't stop him this time either.'

'So you think he can walk through walls?' said Major Sholto.

'He's clever. I can't stop him because I don't know his plan.'

'Solve it then!' said Sholto. 'You're the famous Mr Holmes. Solve the Bainbridge case. How did he do it? Tell me and I'll open the door.'

'Please, James, just let us in!' shouted John. 'This isn't the time for games. You're in danger!'

'You're in danger too while you're here. Please, leave me! Too many of my young men died in Afghanistan. I don't want you three to die as well.'

Sherlock and John had no more ideas. They wanted to help Sholto, but what could they do from the wrong side of the door?

'Solve it, Sherlock!' said Mary. 'Solve the Guard in the Shower case and he'll open the door.'

'But I couldn't solve it before. How can I solve it now?'

'Because it's important now,' said Mary.

Sherlock was angry. What was Mary talking about? She knew nothing about solving crimes.

'She's right!' said John. 'Your mind always works faster when someone's in danger. Well, there's a man in there and he's going to die. Come on, Sherlock! Solve the case!'

Sherlock stopped. Were they right? Was he better at solving things at times like these? He had to try. He thought about Bainbridge, the Guard in the Shower, and he thought about Sholto. What was there about the two men that was the same? The army. And their army uniforms? Were they the same? No. Bainbridge's jacket was red but Sholto's was black. He thought again. What was it? Their belts? Yes, both men had big white belts. Were the belts important?

Suddenly Sherlock thought of a long, very thin knife. The cook in the hotel kitchen had one. When the cook put the knife into some meat, there was no blood. The blood only ran out when the cook took the knife out again.

Sherlock smiled at Mary, and then went back to the door of room 207. 'Major Sholto,' he shouted, 'no one is coming to kill you. Someone has killed you already. It happened a few hours ago.'

'What do you mean?' asked the Major.

'Don't take off your belt,' continued the detective.

'Someone put a thin knife into Bainbridge hours before we saw him. But it was through his belt. He didn't even feel it.'

John was starting to understand. 'So the belt held the wound together. But when Bainbridge took it off, the wound opened.'

'Yes. And by that time, the killer was far away,' said Sherlock.

Now Sholto understood too. But it didn't make any difference to him. 'So I will die in my uniform. That seems a good way to die.' He stood up and moved his good hand towards his belt.

'He solved the case, Major!' called Mary. 'Now you have to open the door. We agreed.'

But Sholto wasn't listening. 'So many good men are already dead,' he said. 'And now it's my turn.' He started to take off the belt.

John was really worried. 'James, don't do it. Stop right now!' he shouted.

But Sholto wanted to talk to Sherlock. 'You and I are the same in many ways, Sherlock,' he said. 'There's a right time to die. You agree, don't you?'

'Of course I do,' said Sherlock.

'And when that time comes, we have to walk towards it bravely.'

'Yes, of course. But not at John Watson's wedding. We don't do that kind of thing, you and I. We don't do that to a friend.'

In the room, Major Sholto closed his eyes.

Outside, John was ready to break down the door.

'No!' said Mary. 'You won't need to do that.'

They waited.

After a moment, they heard the sound of the lock, and slowly the door opened.

A sad smile crossed Sholto's face. 'I think I need a doctor,' he said.

John moved forward to help his friend.

CHAPTER 7
The sign of three

The best man had to dance with a partner in front of all the wedding guests. Sherlock asked Janine to practise with him first. They were in a small room on their own.

'Tell me again. Why are we practising this?' asked Janine.

'Because everyone will see us – and you're a terrible dancer.'

Janine laughed. 'Well, you're a good teacher – and you're a brilliant dancer.'

'I'm going to tell you a secret. I love dancing. I've always loved it. Watch this!' Sherlock did a beautiful turn. 'Dancing doesn't seem to be very useful in crime work, but I'm always hoping for the right case.'

Janine gave Sherlock a long look. 'I've never met anyone like you before.'

'Ah, I almost forgot,' said Sherlock. 'I've found you a nice man. His girlfriend's with him, but she's interested in someone else. He'll be on his own in an hour or two. White jacket, blue shirt. Talk to him.'

Just then, John came into the room and saw Sherlock and Janine together. 'It's good that you've found a girlfriend, Sherlock,' he joked. 'We don't want to remember this wedding only for its murders!'

'One murder,' smiled Sherlock. 'One almost-murder. John always prefers a good story to the facts,' he told Janine.

At that moment, Lestrade arrived. 'I've got him for you,' he said to Sherlock. A man walked into the room behind him.

'Ah! The photographer! Brilliant!' said Sherlock. 'Now, can I look at your camera, please?'

The man seemed a bit frightened.

'What's this about?' he asked. 'I was almost home.'

'Bad luck. You need a faster car,' said Sherlock as he looked at the photos on the camera. 'Ah yes! Very good!'

'What's good?' asked Lestrade.

'You can see for yourself,' said Sherlock as he gave Lestrade the camera.

'Is the murderer in the photos?' asked John.

'Don't look for someone in the photos. Look for the person who isn't in them … isn't in any of them.'

Sherlock waited for someone to speak. John and Lestrade hated Sherlock when he was like this.

'You want everyone else to look stupid,' said John. 'We've talked about this before, Sherlock. It isn't nice.'

Sherlock waited a moment, and then started to explain.

'There's always one person at a wedding who isn't in any photograph. He can go anywhere, and he can carry a big bag with him. And you never even see his face. You only ever see …' Sherlock held the photographer strongly by the arm. '… the camera.'

'What are you doing? What is this?' said the photographer.

'Jonathan Small, today's photographer, is also the Man for One Day. His brother was one of the young men who died in Afghanistan under Major Sholto. He wanted Sholto to die too. He went out with five women when they were working at Sholto's house. Finally he found out the information that he needed: Sholto had an invitation to a wedding. It was the one time that Sholto had to be away from his home and his guards. Small made his plan and practised the murder on Bainbridge. While he took a photo of himself with Bainbridge outside Buckingham Palace, he put a thin knife through the guard's belt and into his back. Bainbridge didn't even feel it, but a few hours later he was almost dead. The same today. While Small was putting people into groups for the photos, he put his knife into Major Sholto's back. Clever. Brilliant, in fact, and his photos are quite good too.'

Sherlock threw Small's mobile to Lestrade.

'This has all the information that you need. You can take him to the police station now.'

'It's not me that you want, Mr Holmes,' said Small. 'Sholto's the killer, not me!' He looked at the floor and said sadly, 'Why didn't I kill him more quickly? Why did I try to be clever?'

'Next time, drive faster!' Sherlock said. Then he took Janine's arm and walked with her to the dance floor.

* * *

John and Mary danced on their own while all their guests watched. Then Sherlock and Janine joined them. After that, Sherlock made another short speech.

'Sorry about earlier,' said Sherlock. 'There was a problem, but we've solved it now. Let's forget about that. Today something much more important has happened: a wedding. And here, in front of you all, I'd like to say: Mary and John, I will always be there for you. Always, for all three of you … I'm sorry, I mean two of you … both … . You know me – I'm not very good at counting. Anyway, now it's time for dancing. Let's have some music. Come on, everyone. Dance!'

While the guests moved onto the dance floor, Sherlock went over to John and Mary.

'Sorry! That was one more piece of detective work than I planned.'

'Detective work?' asked Mary.

'Well, you're always hungry. Your dress is almost too small for you. You don't like the drink that you chose a few weeks ago. And you weren't feeling well this morning. That wasn't because you were worried about the wedding, Mary. All the signs are there.'

'The signs?' Mary asked.

'The signs of three. Mary, you're going to have a child.'

Mary's face broke into a big smile as Sherlock continued, 'You know, the first three months are quite difficult …'

'Sherlock, be quiet!' said John angrily. 'Just don't talk, OK?'

John turned to Mary. 'How did he know that before me? I'm a doctor, but I didn't see the signs. What kind of a husband …?'

'Everything will be fine, John. Stop worrying!' said Sherlock.

'I'm not worrying!' said John.

'I'm the person who's carrying a child,' said Mary. 'I'm worrying!'

'Neither of you must worry,' said Sherlock. 'There's nothing at all for you to worry about.'

'You know nothing about it, Sherlock!' said John.

'Yes, I do. I know that you're already the best parents in the world. You've had lots of practice.'

'What practice?'

'With me, of course!'

They all laughed. Sherlock smiled at his two best friends. Things were changing for them, and maybe their future had less time in it for Sherlock. But he was happy for them.

'Dance!' he said quickly. 'People will see that we're talking. They'll want to know why. Dance!'

'But what about you, Sherlock?' asked Mary.

'We can't all three of us dance together, Mary,' said John. 'There are some things that just don't work as a three.'

Mary knew that he was right. 'Come on then, husband!' she said and pulled John back onto the dance floor.

Sherlock watched them from the middle of the room. As happy people danced and laughed all around him, he suddenly felt very alone. He saw Janine and started to walk towards her. But she was with the man in the white jacket and the blue shirt, and they were clearly enjoying themselves.

Sherlock got his coat. Maybe an interesting case was waiting for him at home.

'Oh, what a night!' sang the band as Sherlock walked to the door. He could still hear the song behind him as he went out into the dark, alone.

THE FAMOUS MR HOLMES

Sherlock Holmes is the world's most famous detective. Since Sir Arthur Conan Doyle's first story about him in 1887, people have read stories about him in 60 different languages. 75 actors have played him in 254 films and TV shows.

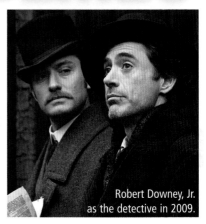

Robert Downey, Jr. as the detective in 2009.

Basil Rathbone played Sherlock Holmes in early films.

Conan Doyle wrote seventy Sherlock Holmes stories. He killed his detective in the thirty-sixth story because he wanted to write about different characters. But later, he wrote more Sherlock Holmes stories. He decided that the detective was only pretending to be dead.

Did you know?

Sir Arthur Conan Doyle was a doctor. He wrote the first Sherlock Holmes story when he didn't have enough work.

He based his detective on one of his teachers at Edinburgh University.

Sherlock, with Benedict Cumberbatch as Sherlock Holmes and Martin Freeman as John Watson, is one of Britain's most popular TV series. But how does the world of Cumberbatch's detective compare with the one that Sir Arthur Conan Doyle wrote about 130 years ago?

Who's your favourite detective from a book, film or TV show? Why?

Conan Doyle's stories

- Holmes uses forensic science – a new idea in the 1880s – to solve crimes.

- Dr Watson works with Holmes and tells readers about their adventures in his diary.

- Watson was a doctor with the British army in Afghanistan in 1880.

- In 'The Sign of the Four', Holmes and Watson help Mary Morstan to find her father. As they work on the case, Watson and Mary fall in love and decide to get married.

The *Sherlock* TV series

- As well as forensic science, Sherlock uses mobile phones and the Internet in his crime work.

- John Watson works with Sherlock and writes a blog about their adventures.

- John was a doctor with the British army in Afghanistan before 2010.

- Mary Morstan is a nurse. She works with John and they fall in love. In 'The Sign of Three', they get married and find out Mary's going to have a child.

What do these words mean? You can use a dictionary.

actor   base on   character   pretend   series   forensic science

CHAPTERS 1-2

Before you read

You can use a dictionary.

1 Match the two halves of the sentences.

    a) A man and woman become husband and wife at **i)** a uniform.

    b) People in the police have to wear **ii)** an army.

    c) People fight for their country when they are in **iii)** a crime.

    d) Killing someone is **iv)** a wedding.

2 Complete the sentences with these words.

    brave case solve speech

    a) She's very … . She isn't frightened of anything!

    b) He's going to make a … to lots of people.

    c) The job of a detective is to … crimes.

    d) That detective is working on a … of Internet crime.

3 Look at 'People and places' on pages 4–5. Which two people …

    a) … live on Baker Street in London?

    b) … are planning their wedding?

    c) … have left the army?

After you read

4 Which sentences are true or false? Correct the false sentences.

    a) Sherlock sends Lestrade text messages because he's in danger.

    b) None of Sholto's men died in Afghanistan.

    c) Sherlock tells Janine things about the men at the wedding.

    d) Archie wants to see Sherlock's wedding photos.

    e) Major Sholto doesn't often leave his house.

    f) Mrs Hudson thinks that things will change for Sherlock after the wedding.

5 Who says this? Who or what are they talking about?

    a) 'It's the most difficult thing that I've ever done.'

    b) 'Today's the big day!'

    c) 'You're going to be very useful.'

    d) 'It's a surprise to see him here.'

CHAPTERS 3-4

Before you read

You can use a dictionary.

6 Choose the correct words.

a hug   your mind   a murder   an obituary   a wound

a) This is information about the life of a dead person.

b) This shows friends and family that you love them.

c) This is the crime of killing someone.

d) If you hurt yourself, you sometimes have this.

e) You think with this.

7 Circle the correct words.

a) It was a very *emotional / logical* day. She couldn't stop crying.

b) *Emotional / Logical* people are often good with computers.

c) The man was carrying a *guard / weapon* – it was a gun.

d) A *guard / weapon* was standing at the door, so they felt safe.

After you read

8 Answer the questions.

a) Why does Sherlock read the emails too quickly?

b) How did Sherlock find out about Bainbridge's case?

c) Where was Bainbridge when Sherlock and John saw him?

d) What did John find out when he moved closer to Bainbridge?

e) Why is the Guard in the Shower case difficult to solve?

9 True or false? What do we know about the Man for One Day?

a) Tessa thinks that he's a ghost.

b) He dated other women in the same week.

c) He had four dates with Tessa.

d) Tessa thinks that he's married.

e) He has had different names.

10 What do you think?

a) How did someone try to kill Bainbridge?

b) Why does Sherlock stop his speech suddenly?

CHAPTER 5

Before you read

11 Do you like weddings? Compare weddings in your country with the wedding in the story. What things are the same? What are different?

12 In Chapter 5, we learn that someone wants to murder a guest at the wedding. What do you think?
   a) Who wants to murder someone?
   b) Which guest does he / she want to kill? Why?

After you read

13 Complete the sentences with these names. You can use names more than once.

Archie   Bainbridge   Lestrade   the Man for One Day   Sherlock   Sholto

   a) … continues his speech because he wants to find …
   b) … leaves the room because he gets a text message from …
   c) … writes a message and gives it to …
   d) … is at the wedding because he wants to murder …
   e) … thinks that the Man for One Day also tried to kill …

14 Choose the correct answers.

   a) Why did the Man for One Day date Tessa?
      i) He wanted to know about John and Mary's wedding.
      ii) He wanted to murder her.
      iii) He wanted to find out about John and Sherlock's work.

   b) Why has the Man for One Day planned a murder at a wedding?
      i) It's an easy place to murder the person.
      ii) It's a difficult place to murder the person.
      iii) It's the only place to murder the person.

   c) Why did the Man for One Day try to kill Bainbridge?
      i) It was a mistake.
      ii) It was a practice.
      iii) He wanted to get into Buckingham Palace.

CHAPTERS 6–7

Before you read

15 What do you think?
   a) What will happen to Major Sholto?
   b) In these chapters Sherlock talks about the 'signs of three'. Who or what are the 'three'?

After you read

16 Put the events in the correct order.
   a) Lestrade takes Small to the police station.
   b) Sholto asks for a doctor.
   c) Sholto goes to his hotel bedroom.
   d) Sholto starts to take off his belt.
   e) Sherlock understands the murderer's plan.
   f) John and Sherlock run after Sholto.
   g) Mary finds Sholto's room.
   h) Lestrade finds the photographer.

17 Answer the questions.
   a) How did the murderer get into the wedding?
   b) Why did he want to murder Sholto?
   c) How did Small try to kill Bainbridge and Sholto?
   d) Why did Sholto and Bainbridge not die?
   e) What news did Sherlock give John and Mary?
   f) How did John and Mary feel about the news?
   g) What happened to Janine?
   h) What did Sherlock do at the end of the story? Why?

18 What do you think?
   a) Sherlock says, 'I never thought that I could be anyone's best friend.' Would you like Sherlock as your friend? Why / Why not?
   b) Small says 'Sholto's the killer, not me.' Is it ever right to kill a killer?

NEW WORDS

What do these words mean?

army (n) ....

belt (n) ....

brave (adj) ....

case (n) ....

crime (n) ....

emotion (n) .... / emotional (adj) ....

guard (n) ....

hug (n) ....

invitation (n) ....

logic (n) .... / logical (adj) ....

mind (n) ....

murder (n & v) .... / murderer (n) ....

nurse (n) ....

obituary (n) ....

solve (v) ....

speech (n) ....

uniform (n) ....

weapon (n) ....

wedding (n) ....

wound (n) ....